The Enchanted Schoolhouse

Also by Ruth Sawyer

ROLLER SKATES

THE YEAR OF JUBILO

THE LONG CHRISTMAS

THE WAY OF THE STORYTELLER

THE CHRISTMAS ANNA ANGEL

JOURNEY CAKE, HO!

THE YEAR OF THE CHRISTMAS DRAGON

By Ruth Sawyer and Emmy Mollès

DIETRICH OF BERNE AND THE DWARF KING LAURIN

The Enchanted Schoolhouse

by RUTH SAWYER

Illustrated by Hugh Troy

The Viking Press · New York

fic

FIC 1. IRISH FAIRY TALES

To my two granddaughters

SALLY and JANE McCLOSKEY

with the wish that each

may find for herself

a brown earthenware teapot

full of enchantment

Contents

The Enchanted Schoolhouse

1. Brian Boru Gallagher

THIS is an Irish tale. Or you might say it is a tale that began in Ireland and about a lad called Brian Boru Gallagher, who had ten years of much knowledge and small courage to him. It began with the brown earthenware teapot that stood on the chimney shelf in the Gallaghers' cabin. It had been fetched from County Kerry to Donegal on the day that Brian Boru's grandmother had married his granda, and it was treasured more than anything at all in the cabin.

Brian Boru had been named for a high King of Ireland in ancient times, a king who had been a great hero and a mighty fighter. As for the lad himself, he had no more fight in his fists than had he been a wee rabbit, and, like a wee rabbit, he took to his heels when anything fierce, like his granda's gander, took after him. You can see for yourself that this Brian Boru Gallagher was no hero at all.

But Tomas Teeney, the schoolmaster, said that Brian was the brightest lad he had ever had in school, that he took to his reading and writing as a blackbird takes to ripe cherries. While the other lads his age were struggling away at their primers, he had read every sign on the roads for five miles around, and every sign on the Donegal railway station, as well as everything that was printed on the boxes of cereals and biscuits in Jamie Donohue's store.

In the Gallaghers' cabin there were no women at all. Four men crowded it, as content as birds in their nest. They were Brian Boru; his father, Timothy; his Uncle Seumas; and his granda, old Timothy. To the lad himself it seemed as if there had never been, nor ever would be, a change in their living, till, without a breath of warning, his Uncle Seumas said one fine evening in the spring, "I do be going to America, to seek my fortune like many an Irishman before me."

The next day he left, saying first to Brian Boru, "When my fortune's made, what shall I be sending you back?"

"Send me something I can be reading."

It took half a year before his Uncle Seumas could get even the toe of his brogans into making a decent living, let alone making a fortune. But with the winter setting in, with the white frost showing on the bogland below the Gallagher cabin, there began to arrive from America a great store of magazines. Up to the time that Willie the post boy began fetching them, a new one every week,

Brian Boru had always lagged at school, to blather away with the master, or borrow a book to be reading. But now, on the day the post arrived, he was the first scholar to cut and run the minute school was let out. He would be away over the bog, up the boreen, as fleet as a wild creature.

Inside the cabin, long after daylight was gone and the candle was lighted, he would spread the magazine on the table and seek through each page to see what was new and what was old inside to enchant him. As he looked, his wonderment grew till he could hold it in no longer. Then he would call to his granda, "Come over, old man that you are, and look at the common things America does be having. Motorcars, every color of the rainbow, that lie along the roads as thick as whin along the bogs—and look at the fine things that do be in every house!"

The pointing fingers, one old and one young, turned the pages together, marking what was printed and what was pictured. And what pictures—as real as if the things themselves lay on the pages!

"Look at the pictures of a city, of a size and splendor to

cover the whole world! On this page there be's snow-white stoves for cooking, with never a sign of turf or coal burning under them. There be's places called bathrooms, with color on the floors and walls as gay as a hummingbird. And look you here, granda—there stands a closet-thing as white as the stove, with the door open so a body can see eatables and drinkables fit for a king."

Old Timothy and his grandson sat spellbound as they pointed to apples as red as hollyberries, oranges as big as their fists, glass bottles holding milk, a cut of ham, a roast of beef. It seemed to them that only enchantment could produce so much food. For in most of the cabins in Donegal a lad knew no more food than could be put on the table at one sitting.

Aloud, this lad spelled the words under the enchanted closet. "Granda—'tis called a r-e-f-r-i-g-e-r-a-t-o-r!"

It was a year to the day from the time his Uncle Seumas had gone to America that his father, Timothy, had been taken with the tinker's itch. Now Irish tinkers are wandering folk, and Timothy was taken suddenly with the itch to be gone somewhere, to see the world—strange places and strange people. He took Brian Boru with him to the Donegal station to see could he get information on cargo boats sailing to foreign ports. He could and he did, and he wrote down the names of several that were sailing from Londonderry and needed men as crew.

The next day brought the post and with it a letter from

Brian's Uncle Seumas. It held so much news that it had to be read by all of them, separately and together. First, he had married a fine Irish-American lass by the name of Delia. They had traveled to a town in the State of Maine, called Lobster Cove, on the Atlantic Ocean. Here he was about to set up in the lobster business—a fine way for a man to make his fortune. The while since, he had paid money down on a sturdy boat and a set of traps. America had fine schools—the best in the world; and he and the lad's new Aunt Delia thought that the lad had better start adventuring himself, see for himself what a grand country America was. Brian Boru could go to school and not pay a shilling for a year of learning.

Inside the letter was a postal order for the passage money.

There was a great blathering among the three of them—would Brian Boru go, or would he *not* go? The lad himself was for staying where he was, where things were familiar and not too grand for a lad his size. Old Timothy thought the Atlantic Ocean was a monstrous big piece of water for the lad to cross alone by himself. It was his father, Timothy, who settled the matter. Did the lad not go, the passage money would have to go back to his Uncle Seumas—a great waste of traveling. Likely there would be a steamer sailing for America the very day he, Timothy, would be shipping aboard his cargo boat; the two of them could journey on the same train to Londonderry. And, for good measure, how could he go traipsing over the world and leave Brian Boru behind to be a burden on his granda?

"Don't blather so much," said old Timothy. "The lad would be more of a blessing than a burden. But I'm thinking he best go. Then we would have three Gallaghers in Donegal who had seen the world. There would not be another cabin in the county would hold the like of that. But I lay a promise on both of ye—ye'll not be gone longer than a year and a day. Promise me that and the lad shall go."

The promise was made, and on the instant Brian Boru felt himself sinking into a bog of despair. How could he leave his granda; how stand up under another master but Tomas Teeney; how find even in America such fine, brave schoolmates as he had here? That made the half of his despair, but what made the other half sank him even deeper. What had he, Brian Boru Gallagher, to take over to America to prove to the lads over there that Ireland was as grand a country as America? He sat crumpled on his creepy stool, while before his eyes swam the pictures from the magazines his Uncle Seumas had sent him. He could hear the American lads scoffing at him.

"Have you motorcars like those, crowding the roads of Ireland, Brian Boru? Have you cities so big and high and wide-spreading, Brian Boru? Have you snow-white stoves that can burn without leave of turf or coal; and have you refrigerators that can hold a feast for a king?"

He groaned a mighty groan.

"What's ailing you?" asked his father.

" 'Tis sunk I am under a great trouble."

"Could your granda or myself be lifting it from you?"

"I'll have to be lifting it myself." Brian Boru gave another groan. He covered his face with his hands and sat so still that he had the other Gallaghers bothered entirely.

At long last the despair broke through him, and he spoke. "Granda, 'tis the pictures in the magazines that Uncle Seumas has been sending from America. You've marked them along with me—the magnificence and the enchantment they do be showing. What in all of Ireland can I be taking across the ocean to show the lads yonder? They'll be laughing and scorning our blessed isle, and the pitifulness of the small things we have in Donegal. 'Tis proud I must be of Ireland if I go to America—and what in all the length and breadth of the land can I be taking with me to hold up my pride?"

Old Timothy pulled his thinking lock and looked sadly at the lad he so greatly loved. "There be's the brown earthenware teapot, your grandmother's own. 'Tis yours now, lad, to take with ye—if it will hold up your pride."

"I'm obliged to you, granda—but where, inside or out, is there magnificence or enchantment in a brown teapot? The lads in America would only laugh at me more." He was about to sink his head in his hands again and let despair pull him down deeper when his eyes settled on the

teapot, standing fine and brave on the chimney shelf. It was the height of a man's hand—a bit more, maybe. And following this sprang the thought—it was just the very height of an Irish fairyman.

He swallowed hard, trying not to let hope get the better of him. But it did. His mind took up the fact that it was spring. Then it went on to skylarks and fairy forts, and fairy thimbles that were just beginning to bloom along the wood thickets on Binn Ban. And from fairy thimbles it went on to primroses—the flower that holds the most enchantment in all of Ireland. He had seen a fine spreading of their gold on the edge of the fairy fort that lay between the Gallagher cabin and the schoolhouse.

His eyes, which had been as dull and dead as chunks of dry turf, suddenly sprang to light. Springtime was fairy time. He had not heard of a single soul in Donegal's seeing a fairy the while since the railroad had been built through from Donegal to Londonderry. But his granda had raised him on tales of the wee people. There was the tale of Conal the piper, who had heard half the tunes he played by sleeping on May Eve on the fairy fort—the very fort Brian Boru passed on his way to school. There was the tale of old Molly Maguire, who was left a piece of fairy gold in thanks for the small piggins of stirabout she had put out for the fairies. He had listened to well-nigh a hundred such tales—and all of them had sprung from the wonder and

enchantment of Irish fairymen. If he could be finding one of those wee men now, and putting him inside the brown teapot for safekeeping, and fetching him to America, he would have something the like of which America could never match.

Clutching hard to his seat on the creepy stool, he asked, "Granda, be's there any fairies at all left in Ireland—in Donegal?"

Old Timothy shook his head. " 'Tis a good fifty years or more since one was seen. I mind the last time I heard of one was when the wee cobbler dropped in to help old Billy Doyle finish the shoes for Brigit's wedding. Brigit Gallagher was your great aunt, and dead these fifteen years."

"And naught other, the least while since?"

"I'm not for sure. But it might have been in the last

famine that a host of wee people filled Cahal Teeney's meal chest—him that was granda to your own schoolmaster."

The next day Brian Boru lagged after school, till he had the master to himself. "Tomas Teeney, sir," he said, "you can lift a deal of trouble from my mind. With May Eve not far off, is there any likelihood of an Irish fairyman being left in yonder fort? And if there be's, what would be the gentlest way of cotching one?"

Tomas Teeney looked Brian Boru well over, from the end of his lugs to the end of his legs. "So that's what has been ailing you, lad, the lee long day! With all the old tales your granda has been telling you, who should know better than yourself that you catch a fairy by the scruff of his neck; that you hold him fast while you snatch the wee red cap from his head. Holding that cap fast you have the power over him. However, I'm thinking, 'twould be a poor way entirely to be treating a wee fairyman. Whatever put the notion into your head?"

Brian Boru told the full of what was on his mind. When the lad had finished, the schoolmaster held him fast by the shoulders, his eyes sharp upon him. "Foreby I can understand you would be wanting something grand to take to America to show the lads over there—something that only Ireland can boast. But if I lend advice and knowledge to you to help find and catch a fairy, I must lay a promise on you, lad. And you must bind yourself to keep it."

"I am bound by the promise," said Brian Boru. "What is it?"

"America, with all its newfangled ways and things, all its magnificence and riches, would be a terribly lonesome spot for a fairyman from County Donegal. I'll give you all the human help I have; but you must promise, after giving the Yankee lads a fine look at him, and maybe giving him a chance to put on them a bit of enchantment, that you then set him free. I'm not one to hold with keeping a linnet in a cage, or any small, wild creature tied fast. Give the fairyman his wee red cap so that he can come home to Ireland and I'll tell you how to catch him."

"I promise," said Brian Boru.

2. The Earthenware Teapot

THAT night Brian Boru spent with the brown earthenware teapot held firmly between his bare knees, and a long length of twine held between his thumb and finger.

"Whatever are you doing, lad?" asked old Timothy.

"Fixing the lid of the teapot so it will not be losing itself on the way to America."

"By this and by that I see you are content to go, and feel no shame to your pride."

"Content is what I am, if by this and by that I fetch with me what I hope to fetch."

"You're blathering nonsense. Didn't I tell you you could be fetching the brown teapot?"

His granda never caught the sparkle in the lad's eyes; all he saw was the nodding of his head over the twine and the lid. Before the tying was finished, Brian Boru's father, Timothy, came back from the Donegal station and held a length of printed paper under the lad's nose. " 'Tis your passage to America. We sail from Londonderry on the same day—the first of May."

For the moment there was no sound in the cabin but the sifting of turf ash to the hearth. Then Brian Boru gave a sigh as long as the silence. The sparkle was still in his eyes as he answered, " 'Twill be a grand day to sail, I'm thinking. Foreby, 'twill leave me home for May Eve."

The schoolmaster had told Brian Boru that the best time—in fact, the only possible time—to catch a fairyman would be May Eve. He was very insistent about it. If there were any fairies at all left in Donegal—after the building of the railroad, and the fetching of Yankee cornmeal to Ireland, and the coming of airplanes with bombs in them during the last war—May Eve would have to be the time to see them. That night alone would fetch a fairyman out of the fairy fort. This, and the rest that Tomas Teeney had told him, Brian Boru kept to himself.

Long before May Eve came, Brian Boru had taken a fine gander around the fairy fort, that he might mark well the place he had been told to watch. He found the blackthorn at one corner, and the stalk of buchaleen-bwee—the tall mullein—near it, with just a narrow space between, where he could lie, scrooched close to the ground. It was a fine thing, Tomas Teeney had said, that May Eve came at the dark of the moon. A solitary fairy would have little fear of leaving the fort in the dark, with no moonlight to betray him. What was more, the lad would cast no shadow to betray himself.

On the night itself the lad found he had small mice scampering inside his stomach. So full he was with fear he could eat no supper. If he had never known for a certainty that he was no hero, that he had no strength to his fists and no bravery in his heart, he knew it now. He crawled into the outshot bed he shared with his father and lay with his eyes clamped shut, as wide awake as a nightwalker. So he lay, without a stir or a twist to him, till the other Gallaghers had gone to bed, the candle had been blown out, and there was a fine sound of snoring filling the cabin. It took a deal of care and caution to step over his sleeping father, to reach the floor, to pull on his pants, shirt, and jacket, to lift the lid of the door and open it without a creak to it.

Once outside, he took to shivering—not with the cold, but with the dark. Even a scant mile to travel at the dark of the moon, down a boreen, snagging a corner of the bog, and on to the edge of the fort, took a sight more courage than Brian Boru had ever had in his entire life.

So many times in the last three years had his bare feet

felt their way to school and back again that it took no searching for them now to follow the blind track they had made. The brown teapot Brian Boru held tightly against his stomach, where the mice still scampered. Every foot of the journey was fearsome. His heart thumped so hard against the teapot that it rattled the lid, and his teeth chattered as if every one was loose in his head.

I'll be shaking myself to bits before the night's half gone, he thought—and then he found the place between the mullein stalk and the blackthorn, and he dropped to the ground like a dead bag of bones.

At first he could see nothing at all. Then he could make out the fringe of the thornbush, and, on the other side, the mullein stalk shooting up against the black sky with two stars atop it. He reached out one hand and found that he could almost touch the mullein.

The words of the schoolmaster came back to him, to lay a quieting touch on his heart. "Listen, lad, should a fairy-man come out of the fort, he'll be coming for a single purpose—to ride out into the night to join the lost fairy host, wherever they may be. So the first thing he will do is to make straight for the buchaleen-bwee. He will bend it down low so as to throw his wee leg over it. The instant he does this, the mullein stalk will turn into a fairy pony. So you must catch him on the instant, before the two of them are gone."

A sleepy bird chirped from the whin. Somewhere from

the wood thicket on Binn Ban an owl hooted. These were
natural sounds—but what manner of sound would a fairyman make?

Brian Boru raised his head and looked as far as the darkness let him. Across the smooth green grass that covered
the fort he could make out neither sight nor sound. He had
placed the teapot close to his hand; now he remembered
he had not freed the lid. Carefully he unknotted the twine
and put the teapot back on the ground beside him. Time
lagged. A minute could be as long as an hour. How much
waiting did a lad have to do before a solitary fairy took

it into his head to come atop green earth on May Eve?

A high, whistling note, thin as a throstle's, caught Brian Boru's ear. It sounded like a bird, and yet not like a bird— at least not like any bird Brian Boru had ever heard. Upward he craned his neck. In that instant the whole of the adventure might have been ruined. For as the whistling came nearer it sounded as if it were coming from close to the ground, as if some wee thing were coming through the close-cropped grass. What was more, it was coming toward the very spot where the lad lay. It was this that almost jumped Brian Boru to his feet—which would have upset the

teapot with a clatter and set whatever was abroad away
and back into the night again. Out of the darkness, not the
height of a man's hand from the ground, appeared the
small wee figure of a man, strutting as proudly as a
bantam cock.

Brian Boru took a fast hold on himself. Not a twist or a

twiggit did he make. He lay watching and listening while the whistle mounted into the air and the wee man strutted toward the high mullein stalk. "How do you cotch a fairyman?" Brian Boru had asked the schoolmaster a while since. After the next moment, when it was all over, he could never have told. But cotch him he did, before ever the man's wee leg had been thrown over the mullein, before ever the mullein had become an enchanted pony. All the lad knew was that he was on his two feet, one hand holding the fairyman by the scruff of his neck while the other snatched the red cap from the wee man's head, and that his ears were filled with the sound of loud lamenting.

Such a wriggling and such a wailing the fairyman put up. "Laddy, laddy, however have ye the heart to thieve my cap, and the bad manners to be holding me like a new-born cat!" His wee face was scrooched up into a sour smile while he went on pleading. "Whatever good can come of your bad behavior? Put me down, put the wee red cap back on me head, and I'll show you where the last crock of fairy gold be's hidden."

"I'm not wanting gold. Where you and I do be going, fairyman, they have gold aplenty."

"Then turn me loose, laddy. I have no heart to be going anywhere but here. I will grant ye a wish—any wish at all."

"Having cotched you, I have my wish. Now into the brown teapot you go. Tomorrow we sail for America. When we get there, we'll be showing the lads and lasses of the richest country on earth that there be's something Ireland has with more enchantment and wonder than anything at all they can picture in their magazines."

"Meaning myself?"

"Meaning yourself."

Even in the darkness Brian Boru could see that the fairyman was near to crying. His face was creased into woe like a withered hazelnut. How could the lad ever shut him up in a teapot and tie the lid hard down on him! It was worse than caging a linnet.

Brian Boru remembered the promise he had made Tomas Teeney. Now he spoke it again to the fairyman. "If you

will come with me quiet-like, I promise to set you free as bird, to come back to Donegal and Ireland. You shall have your red cap tight on your head, and be free as a skylark."

The fairyman scrooched his head down to take a good look at Brian Boru's face. "Are you a lad of honor?"

"I am that. Now into the teapot you go—and not a squirm or a whistle out of you."

The wee man fitted in, with room to spare. As the lid was fastened on, with much twisting of twine and tying of knots, the lad said, "You'll get air aplenty down the spout. I'll see you have griddle bread with currants in it, and some cheese, to stay your wee stomach. Here's wishing a safe journey to the two of us."

The next day Timothy Gallagher shipped out of Londonderry on his cargo boat to ports unknown, and Brian Boru, with his telescope bag in one hand and the brown earthenware teapot in the other, walked up the gangplank to the steamer that was to fetch him to America. The small mice were back in his stomach. He took a fast hold on his courage and tried to grin at the steward who took his bag from him and said, "Welcome aboard, lad. Might this be your first crossing?"

"Crossing what?"

"What but the Atlantic Ocean?"

"It is that. And by the size of the ship and the size of the waves already rocking it, and by the feelings inside my stomach, I am wishing this minute I may never be crossing any ocean—never again!"

Suddenly a fear sprang at him. Never could he stand the burden of so much misery, homesickness, strangeness all about him, if his grand intentions for himself and America failed. He clamped his hand hard over his bony chest to feel if the wee red cap was still safe where he had pinned it to his shirt the night before with a thorn from the

blackthorn. It was. The end of the thorn scratched against his skin, and the cap, small as it was, made a lump he could just feel. This picked up his courage a bit.

He followed the steward down a companionway into the steerage. There was less weight to his feet and his heart as he walked the narrow corridor. The depth of the ship gave out strange smells. He straightened his shoulders and felt a sudden lifting of pride within him. After all was said and done, had not Irish lads been coming to America since the first of the bad famines, nearly two hundred years ago? And had not every one of them stepped forth like the King of Ireland's son himself, ready to meet whatever adventure faced him along the way? Pride, a stout heart, and a fairyman in a brown teapot made as fine traveling companions as a lad could wish for.

3. Brian Boru Crosses the Atlantic Ocean

BRIAN BORU discovered that he was born to the sea. The scampering mice were gone from his stomach—for good, he hoped. The highest seas and the stormiest winds, which set the small steamer rocking like a low-swung cradle, had no effect on his spirits or his appetite. He found the steward to his liking, and before they were two days gone they had become as good friends as himself and Tomas Teeney—almost.

The ship not being crowded, Brian Boru had a cabin to himself—and a good thing it was. For he could let the fairyman out three times a day to stretch his legs, doing amazing acrobatics around the cabin. On the wall, beside the lower berth, a small string hammock hung, for putting odds and ends of a traveler's belongings in. But here the fairyman loved to stretch out, his hands back of his head, his legs crossed, eying Brian Boru with an impish grin. They held long conversations together about this and that, for, as the fairyman said, " 'Tis not often, lad, that fairy and mortal cross an ocean together."

Day and night Brian Boru wore the shirt with the red cap pinned to it; it never left his back. And wherever he went, he carried the teapot with him.

"Are you never free of that teapot?" asked the steward, who was a County Derry man himself.

" 'Tis a keepsake. 'Tis an heirloom. I have my granda promised to return in a year and a day, fetching the teapot back with me sound and whole."

"Can you not be filling your stomach at the table without always fetching away with you milk or a scone or a slab of queen's cake?" asked the steward.

"I cannot," said Brian Boru. " 'Tis time I put on weight and strength to measure up to my namesake, the mighty King Brian Boru."

The truth was that he had the fairyman to feed; and that small, wee person had grown a tremendous appetite from the sea air and the life of leisure he was living. Always, when he heard the door of the cabin open and had made sure that it was the lad, he would be putting his lips to the inside of the spout and shouting, "The sides of my stomach are scraping each other with hunger. What have ye fit for a fairyman to eat?"

They had been less than two days at sea before both lad

and fairy had acquired a prodigious taste for ice cream. Never had the fairyman tasted it before; but the lad had had a rare treat of it a few times in his life, when his father had brought him a slab from the ice cream peddler at the Donegal station, whose cry was,

> Icy cream a penny a lump,
> The more you eat, the more you jump.

At first Brian Boru had two troubles—the trouble of getting the steward to serve him a second dish to take to his cabin, and the trouble of getting the fairyman to taste it. Putting a bit on the tip of a teaspoon, he would say coaxingly, "Lay your small pink tongue to it and get the flavor."

Whereupon the fairyman would lay his tongue to the ice cream, lap it twice or thrice, and then lay a hand to his stomach, saying, "It makes my shirt ache, laddy."

"Try again. Try till you get the urge for it," the lad would coax; and at long last, the small wee man got an oversized appetite for the ice cream, till he had a longing for it almost as big as Brian Boru's own. They tried all flavors, and liked chocolate the most, and by the end of the voyage the fairyman could eat the best of a dishful.

Once the lad eyed him with troubled eyes and said, "Curb your taste, wee man that you are, or you'll be outgrowing the teapot. Then howsomever will I be fetching you to America?"

There were moments on the voyage that were not all ice cream and queen's cake. Brian Boru felt for the first time in his life a great heart hunger—for his granda, for Donegal, and for the schoolmaster. He loved the small white schoolhouse, with fuchsias climbing its front and the bed of wild flowers that Tomas Teeney had coaxed his scholars to bring from the wood thicket; he loved the bogs by the roadside and the plants under the windows and around the doorstep. America might have far finer schoolhouses—he never doubted it—but the one where he had learned his three R's was part of his life. He thought of his father, Timothy, and wondered often how he was faring.

But the steward from County Derry had children of his own, and on those days when he guessed that the lad was homesick and down-daunted he would find time to go up on deck with him and tell him of his voyages and of some of the strange lands he had voyaged to. On stormy days he took him all over the ship, from the captain's bridge and the first-class quarters down to the engine room and the galleys; and he made Brian Boru acquainted with every Irishman who had shipped as crew.

"Here's a lad from Donegal. He's crossing the Atlantic by himself, along with a big brown teapot. Brian Boru, shake hands with Jamie O'Neil from County Cork." And so it went, until the lad picked up heart again.

Evenings in his cabin, with the door safely bolted, he would let the fairyman out; and after a fine stretching of his legs the wee man would perch on the side of the twine hammock while Brian Boru stretched himself out on the bunk.

Then began a fine telling of tales between the two, all beginning the good Irish way—"Here's a tale as long as I can tell you and twice as long as you can tell me." They matched tale for tale, the lad telling those he had had from his granda, and the fairyman telling some of the strange happenings in and out of the fairy fort that he could remember.

At the end of such a tale the lad would always ask, "How many years ago would you say it all might be happening?"

And the fairyman would answer always the same, "A hundred or more, maybe, laddy."

" 'Tis a great age you have on you," Brian Boru said once.

And the fairyman had answered that with, "Long enough

to know which is the finest country in all the world to be living. 'Tis back there I am wishing myself this minute." The lad said nothing, but it was a bit of comfort to know that the fairyman had homesickness as well as himself.

The ending of the voyage was never to be forgotten. After fair days and foul, after high seas and calm, after sleeping in his shirt for too long and wishing he could strip it off him and take a good scrubbing, Brian Boru watched the ship come to anchor in the harbor and wait for the tug to bring the pilot aboard. For it was the pilot who would take the ship in, and safely up to the waiting dock.

Leaning over the rail beside the steward, and clutching fast to the teapot, the lad watched the crew drop the rope ladder over the side and the small spry figure of the pilot climb it and, with barely a nod at those watching him, make for the captain's bridge. During the sail up the harbor, with the towering skyscrapers showing up sharp and jagged against a bright midday sky, Brian Boru stood spellbound. The city was all the pictures had promised— a giant of a city! He hoped his Uncle Seumas would not forget to meet him on the dock, and he hoped he would show him a small piece of the city. Last of all, Brian Boru took a firm grip of his courage and hoped he would not be scared at whatever he might be seeing.

After the steward left him, and he stood quite alone, he even untied the lid of the teapot to let the fairyman get a gander at the skyscrapers.

Out of the teapot was thrust the small wee head. One look at the vastness of it all, and, with a soft whimpering, the fairyman scrooched back down into the bottom. "Laddy, laddy, let me loose. This is no country to be coming to. All the wizards in the world must have made it."

Brian Boru fastened the lid tight again, with many knots and twists to hold it, so he could give his whole attention to watching the crowd gathered on the dock and try could he see his Uncle Seumas's among the many eager, up-turned faces. As the ship eased closer, and the crew stood ready to catch the hawsers, the lad still failed to find the familiar face. Whatever would he do, a stray lad in a strange country, with no one to claim him? In all the fashing and blather the three Gallaghers had had over his coming to America, such a happening had never come into the minds of any of them. The lad waited, any moment expecting the scampering mice back in his stomach again.

Suddenly a shouting voice reached him. In the midst of the crowd a hand was thrust high, waving wildly. "Brian—Brian Boru! I'm here to welcome you!" It was his Uncle Seumas!

His own hand waved back. His own voice shouted, "I'm here myself, Uncle Seumas, thankful for your welcome!"

After that he waited his turn, up the companionway, down the gangplank. The last thing he did before taking a firm grip of his telescope bag was to whisper down the spout of the teapot, "Whatever you do—whatever happens outside—rest you quiet, wee man."

Brian Boru was proud of his Uncle Seumas. He was every inch an Irishman; in no way had America, with all its magnificence, pushed down on him. He took the tele-scope bag, and Brian Boru tagged him over to where a big man in a uniform stood under a sign marked CUSTOMS. In a grand manner his Uncle Seumas presented the bag and said, "Inspector, do you care to open this piece of luggage brought over by my nephew?"

The inspector sniffed and swept the telescope bag aside. For a moment it looked as if that was all there was to the thing called "Customs"; but, before the moment was over and done with, the inspector's eye caught the brown earthenware teapot. "Boy, come here! What are you carrying away with you?"

" 'Tis naught at all but my mother's teapot, which likely the lad has fetched over as a present from the old country," said his uncle.

"It has the lid fastened on with great care. The boy could be smuggling in contraband for someone—yourself, perhaps," said the inspector.

Brian Boru's heart stood still. "Contraband" was a word he had never met till that moment. It sounded as if it could mean terrible things. And how was he knowing that it might not be another name for an Irish fairyman? If the man scowling down at him made him untie the knots and lift the lid, all was lost. He did his best to keep his lips from fluttering like poplar leaves. He tried to speak his words bravely.

"I'd not have my grandmother's teapot with a broken lid. So I made it fast for the journey. You can shake it if you like, but you'll hear naught inside of it." He kept his hand steady as he held out the teapot. Then a better notion caught at him. "I'll shake it for you, sir, and all you need do is to listen." Making a silent prayer that the fairyman would hold fast, he gave the teapot a mighty shake.

Not a sound came out of it, and the lad's heart began galloping with hope. For a lee long time the black eyes of the inspector bored into the blue ones of the lad. At last came another sweep of the hand and a harsh-sounding "Move on, the two of you."

The three of us, thought Brian Boru.

4. Brian Boru and the Biggest City

THE SHIP from Londonderry docked at noon, and the rest of the day was as full of wonderment as griddle bread is full of currants. Brian Boru and his Uncle Seumas took a bus to a place called an Automat, where they had their dinner. Not one of the magazines his Uncle Seumas had sent him had had a picture of such enchantment. The lad's pocket was filled with nickels, and around the walls of the big place he went, to push one nickel in one slot, maybe two in another, and perhaps even more in a third, so that out from the spots in the wall came eatables and drinkables —all one could hold! At the last he found the slots for chocolate ice cream, and he pushed for two dishes. He ate one of them; then, taking the other along with the brown teapot, he found a door marked GENTLEMEN, and inside, in a dark corner, he fed the dish to the fairyman.

He said, "Wee small man, it's proud of you I am this day. You had the uniformed person called an inspector fooled entirely."

After that they rode on the top of the bus to Central Park Zoo. The wonders of the shop windows they passed equaled anything Brian Boru had seen in the magazines, and so did the parade of motorcars—"All colors of the rainbow"—which swept past them. High buildings towered over them.

His Uncle Seumas pointed out this and that. "Yonder is St. Patrick's Cathedral—one of the finest. Across and above is one of the many fine banks where they do keep hidden millions of dollars, just for the devilment of it. That's Tiffany's, as full of jewels as the queen's crown, and one of the richest stores in all the world."

Brian Boru could see those very jewels sparkling at him

from one of the windows. He clutched the teapot tighter
to him. He would need all the enchantment the fairyman
could lay on the place where his uncle lived and where he
would be going to school to offset the enchantment of the
great city he had already laid his two eyes to.

The zoo was a place that passed all imagining. What
Brian Boru liked best were the bright-colored birds, the

monkeys, and the seals. The seals barked just like a kennel-ful of dogs; and when their keeper came with fish to feed them they put on a regular performance, jumping and slid-ing and diving and catching and making monkeyshines—more than the monkeys made.

Whenever the noise was greatest and he had the chance, Brian Boru would put his lips to the teapot's spout and whisper, "Keep up a stout heart, wee man. Tonight, accord-ing to my Uncle Seumas, we take a train to Lobster Cove, with no more noise of crowding to the place than we have in Donegal. And I promise, you'll have your wee red cap back in the whisk of a cat's tail."

They rode in a subway for miles, and came up out of it

for all the world like a parcel of rabbits coming out of their warrens. Not too far distant was what was called a "supermarket." They went inside, and the bigness of it took Brian Boru's breath away. Ten and more of Jamie Donohue's store in Donegal could have fitted neatly inside it.

There were wire baskets on wheels, to put your stuff into. The lad saw people pushing these around filled and brimming over. His uncle shoved the handle of one into his hands.

"And what do I do with it, except I give the teapot a ride in it?" Brian Boru asked.

His uncle put more nickels and dimes into the lad's pocket. "Up and down the aisles you go, till you see something you like. Then you help yourself to it."

"And if I'm caught twigging, then what?" And he repeated a rhyme he had learned when he was very young.

"He who twigs what isn't hisn,
If he's cotched he goes to prison."

"You'll not get by without paying. Now get going, laddy, and you will be seeing enough food to fill the stomachs of the folk in Donegal for more than a year."

There were rows of things in cans, and more in boxes—biscuits and the like. There was a great spreading out of fruit—apples the color of hollyberries and oranges as big as your fist. Brian Boru helped himself to six of each kind.

He picked out a box of sweet biscuits called "fig newtons" and a package labeled "vanilla wafers." From the pictures they looked good. He went on to the place filled with cheese and picked out a small round one wrapped up in shining red paper.

Suddenly he remembered that he had a new Aunt Delia and inquired politely, "Would she like something out of the store that has Jamie Donohue's beaten to a pulp?"

"Your Aunt Delia has a sweet tooth. You might get her one of those packages of caramels and a box of chocolates."

They finished the day by going to the top of the Empire State Building. They rode up in what was called an "elevator." It started the mice scampering inside Brian Boru's stomach. It was the last time he was to feel them, that instant when the cage-thing left the earth and soared up and up and up, till it had a small lad who had no bravery to him turned almost inside out. After the sixth floor he gripped his Uncle Seumas's hand. On the top, towering over the city, he tried being an owl and looking all ways at once. He saw spires of gold, bridges over the rivers, boats that looked the size of beetles, and one airplane that flew close enough for him to see people sitting in the round windows. At one window, a lady waved her hand to him. What a day—what a day!

That night he slept on the train, sitting bolt upright at first, until he was shown how something could be pulled out and the seat leaned backward, leaving a lad half lying

down. He had the seat next to the window, and soon his Uncle Seumas was asleep and Brian Boru was free to slip the lid off the teapot.

"Are you dead or alive?" he asked, speaking low.

"A bit of both," was the answer. "Can I venture out and stretch my legs?"

"You can venture. Sit close to the teapot, and I'll give you something to eat." The fairyman supped late on vanilla wafers and an apple. "How are you liking America?" the lad asked.

" 'Tis not any of it I'm liking. You can have it all to yourself. My ears are exploding with noises, my shins are blue with dandering about—and were it not for the ice cream I would be afeard to live through another night, into another day."

"Cheer up, wee man, you'll be in a fine, fair place to-morrow."

And that they were!

5. Lobster Cove—and a Refrigerator!

THEY woke to a country of green trees, of blue skies, of smooth roads with tidy cottages, two stories high, bordering them.

Waiting for them at the station was a fine new truck, which they climbed into, and his Uncle Seumas drove a shortish distance to the cove. There were tall red brick chimneys on the cottages; the pasture land was lush with grass and thick with cows. The barnyards had themselves full of chickens and pigs.

While Brian Boru was still full of wonderment at the tidiness all about him, his uncle swung the truck into a dooryard, and there, in the doorway, was his new Aunt Delia to welcome him. She was young and pretty, with cheeks just the color of the thornbloom.

"Find me a prettier lass anywhere," said his Uncle Seumas proudly.

Never had Brian Boru been hugged so tight, nor had he had so many kisses given him. Inside the kitchen he put the teapot down for an instant to reach into the paper bag he had been carrying as well, all the way from the supermarket—and thrust out the caramels and chocolates, mumbling, "A present for yourself, Aunt Delia."

That made a fine beginning. There was a fine breakfast —his first taste of American bacon, which was crisp and flavorsome. The eggs were done in a pudding, which his Aunt Delia called "scrambled." There were hot muffins and good jam to spread on them, and all the milk he could drink. But as they ate, and blathered about the old country, Brian Boru's eyes filled as full of new things as his stomach. For the kitchen was as pretty as a picture, and square against one wall stood a *refrigerator!* The meal over, Brian Boru asked could he look inside. What he saw there was no disappointment: eggs where they should be, milk in glass bottles, a cut of ham. And he had the great

satisfaction of putting his five apples and six oranges on the shelf where they had belonged in the picture.

That done, he gathered up the brown teapot and asked politely where might his bed be.

"Your Aunt Delia will show you. But leave that teapot in the kitchen. Your Aunt Delia will put it on a shelf. 'Tis my own mother's, Delia lass."

For an instant Brian Boru looked with terrified eyes on his uncle. His words were stuttered, so great was his scaring. "Granda gave the teapot to me. He knew I wanted something fine to show the lads of America, and something belonging to me to lift the homesickness from the long journey. I still have some of it, so I'll be keeping the brown teapot close with me till I am cured of it."

For a moment his uncle looked at him with rare puzzlement. Then he laughed. "By all means, laddy, keep it. Now I must be off to the lobster traps. Your Aunt Delia will show you what a fine room she has been fixing for your own self."

Here again was wonderment. Instead of living, eating, sleeping, and cooking in the one room of the cabin, here you went up to a second floor, where you slept. And up here there was one of those places in the magazines called a "bathroom." His Uncle Seumas had one! Brian Boru would take his time and look it over so his Aunt Delia would never know how green he was in an American house.

His room was fine and fancy—too fancy for him. It had windows with lace curtains and a bed with a spread on it instead of a quilt. There was a chest to put his things in; and one drawer of it his Aunt Delia pulled out. She pointed inside. "Your Uncle Seumas put a few things in here for you to wear. He knew you would be wanting to wear the same things the American boys wear."

He thanked her. He stood, first on one foot, then on the other, waiting for her to go. She must have been a very knowledgeable girl, for if he had put it into words she could never have got the idea sooner. She was out the door and down the stairs in no time, and Brian Boru undid the knots and slipped the lid off the teapot.

"Come out, wee man. You can have the run of the room. There be's a closet to hide in. There be's a chest to sleep in. By the way that my Aunt Delia eyed the teapot, you'd best keep out of it. What have you to say for yourself?"

The fairyman pulled himself up and out, and sat on the edge of the teapot, letting his feet dangle over the side. "I am in as many knots as the twine you just dropped on the floor." He gave Brian Boru a long gander, then slowly winked one eye. "I'm thinking 'tis nearly a castle your uncle has. I never saw a fisherman of any sort in Ireland living in such grandeur. Maybe by way of holding our luck we'd best give three hurrahs for America."

It was the end of the week when Brian Boru and his brown teapot arrived at Lobster Cove, which left him a fine Saturday and Sunday to get acquainted with the new home, the country around it, and the bay that stretched out from the cove and went spreading for a dozen miles before it opened into the Atlantic Ocean.

Early both mornings, after a fine breakfast of ham and eggs and lemon pie, he went out on the lobster boat with his Uncle Seumas. He wished he had eyes at the back of his head as well as forward, there were so many things to see and learn about a boat and the lobsters.

His Uncle Seumas had one other man aboard, who was first mate and helper. His name was Jim Matthews. He looked as thin and strong as a fishing pole, and he chewed on the stem of an old pipe that was as empty as a last year's birds' nest. He paid no attention to Brian Boru until they swung around Bean's Island. Then he took out a sack of tobacco, filled and lighted his pipe, took a good look at Brian Boru, and said, "If you aim to make yourself handy on the boat, take this second boathook and stand by me, ready to give a hand with the traps."

His uncle slewed the boat suddenly around a wooden buoy that bobbed on the choppy surface of the bay. Jim Matthews suddenly thrust his hook out, caught the buoy, flung it into the cockpit, and started hauling up on a rope. Brian Boru stood in great puzzlement, watching for what might be at the other end. A couple of minutes and his

curiosity was satisfied. An oblong boxlike thing made of lattice broke the surface of the water, spilling seaweed and water into the boat as Jim pulled it over the stern. From inside came a great sound of flapping, and through the slats Brian Boru could see some strange greenish creatures.

"Would you be calling them lobsters?" he asked.

"If they hain't, boy, then the world is made of green cheese." Jim Matthews opened up a door that ran along the top side of the trap. Very carefully he reached in, caught one of the creatures halfway between its head and tail, and lifted it out. The lad could see that it had great claws—strong enough, maybe, to crush a finger. Deftly the mate gripped one claw tightly, while from his pocket he drew a small wooden wedge and slipped it into a break in the shell of the claws; then he did the same thing with the second claw.

"That fixes the son-of-a-gun. A baby could play with it now. Want to take hold of it, boy, and get your first good look at a Maine lobster?"

That was the last thing Brian Boru wanted to do. He saw the lobster being thrust at him and the mate's sharp eyes looking him over. What could an Irish lad do but try to match the courage of any American lad? He reached out his hand and took the terrible creature. What was more, he hung on to it, although the claws waved about as if ready to take a bite of his hand. Then he saw that the wedges had shut and fastened the claws tight; and all the creature could do was to swing them and flap its tail with madness.

Feeling more courage, Brian Boru began to look the creature over, and he found it altogether amazing. It had two long antennae, like the butterflies had—some of them at least. The eyes were black as beads and stood out a goodish distance from its head. The green of its shell was mottled, and its tail was put together like a train of cars, in sections.

"When you're through studying the old feller, put him inside the cabin—you'll see the crate for the lobsters. Then come back for a hunk of seaweed to put over them," said Jim Matthews.

That began the makings of Brian Boru into a lobster-man, or at least into an apprentice. Before another morning had gone, he had steered the boat, learning just where to slow down as they neared the traps. It took him almost till summer before he had learned the knack of putting the wedges in the claws. But in no time at all he learned to

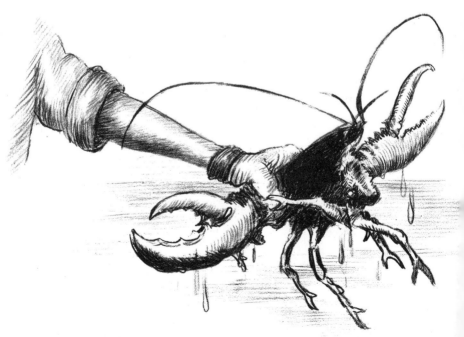

steer a good course, taking the sea, when it was rough
and the waves high, at the right angle, learning quickly to
slip fish for bait on the wooden skewer inside each trap,
getting the hang of catching a buoy with the boathook
and pulling it over the side while Jim caught the rope and
began hauling. Lobstering was a fine business, except in
cold weather, and Brian Boru hoped that his Uncle Seumas
would make his fortune at it.

Those first two days Brian Boru's uncle said the lad
had brought him luck—the real luck of the Irish. They
caught more lobsters than had been caught before in a
full week's fishing. What was more, that first night Brian
Boru tasted his first mess of boiled lobster; and nothing
so far that he had seen in any of the magazine pictures
could have equaled the flavor and tenderness and delight.

When he was almost through his second one he suddenly stopped and asked, "Uncle, would you and my Aunt
Delia take any offense if I put by the meat of the tail to
eat sometime later? I have a way of getting hungry in the
middle of the night."

Seumas Gallagher laughed. "Your aunt and myself took
the notion we heard you creep down to the refrigerator
last night and help yourself to what Americans call a
'snack.' What's in the house is yours, lad, so long as you
bide with us."

Brian Boru waited until sleep seemed to have wrapped
the whole house in safe quiet. He had dozed twice; and

the last time it had taken a hard tugging of the fairyman on the lug of one ear to waken him.

"Laddy, laddy, are you forgetting entirely? My stomach is as empty as the teapot, now I am out of it."

It was a grand feast the fairyman had—himself taking as great a fancy to Maine lobster as the lad. To go with it were some fresh-baked rolls, jam, a small mug of milk, and a wedge of mince pie. What the fairyman could not eat, the lad finished with gusto.

" 'Tis a grand country, this United States of America," Brian Boru said on a full stomach.

"I'm thinking the same," said the fairyman. " 'Twill not be such a hardship after all to see a bit more of it. How often do you think your Aunt Delia will be having lobster for tea?"

6. The School at the Cove

IN SPITE of the sun, late May could be as cool in Maine as it was in Donegal. His Uncle Seumas had to waken Brian Boru that Monday morning, and he stood by to see that the lad got into the wool shirt, the blue jeans, sneakers, and sweater, and looked right for his first day at school—an American school.

Suddenly Brian Boru had small appetite for his breakfast. But by the time the school bus picked him up, his Aunt Delia had filled a fine lunchbox for him, and she wished him luck. He needed it, for in the bus the Lobster Cove boys and girls looked him over with as much curiosity as he had shown with his first lobster. And when they all spilled into the schoolyard, Brian Boru was wishing himself back in Ireland, along with the fairyman and all his enchantment. How ever had he thought he would have the courage to face a strange country, a strange school, and at least fifty strange schoolmates! He knew exactly how a lobster must feel with its claws plugged and no protection to it.

Something quick and terrifying was taking hold of his feet. He was on the point of taking to his heels and running, running, running. The direction did not matter a farthing as long as he could put distance between himself and all this strangeness.

Then it was he caught his first real gander at the schoolhouse and the yard. That fastened him firmly to the earth beneath him. For the schoolhouse was stricken with the look of poverty and ugliness. A dirty yellow it was, with sagging doorsteps, and nothing planted around it to make it gay and pretty. He thought of the fresh whitewashed schoolhouse on the side of Binn Ban, the fuchsias climbing it, the flowers edging the windows and sprinkling the yard, green and tidy. Here not so much as a spear of grass showed. It was strange that this should give him courage. It began in his stomach, and widened the spread of his shoulders, and stiffened his knees, and showed through the blue of his two eyes, so that he could look any lad or lass in the face and say, "I'm Seumas Gallagher's lad—and I come from Ireland." There was pride in every word.

A voice at his back said, "Seumas Gallagher's lad is welcome. Come inside and I'll get you registered."

Brian Boru turned on his heel and saw a woman. She was as young and pretty as his Aunt Delia—almost. But

she was too old to be a scholar; there was but one thing else she could be—the schoolmistress. It took him completely by surprise.

Very politely he said, "Do they not be having schoolmasters in America?"

"They do indeed. The older boys and girls here have a schoolmaster, but I rather think you're going to be in my room."

Inside, in the room below, where the third and fourth graders were, it looked as dreary and forlorn as the outside had promised. The desks and seats were chipped, ink-stained, and sagging; the windows were bleary-eyed. Not a bright spot in the whole room. He stood beside the

teacher's desk and with but half his wits gave his age—
ten; his birthplace—Carn-a-ween, County Donegal, Ireland; his full name—Brian Boru Gallagher; and added
proudly, "My father named me after an Irish king and a
great hero!"

"Fine. We'll expect great things of you, Brian. My name
is Katie Joy, and I was named after a great-aunt who
helped to settle Lobster Cove." The schoolmistress smiled
at him, and Brian Boru knew that they would be friends.
"We'll start you off in the third grade, and see where you
belong."

Before the week was over and done with, both Katie
Joy and the teacher of the three upper grades—Peter
Haskins—were at their wits' end to find out where he did
belong. He did his figures and spelling with the fourth
grade; he climbed the stairs and did his writing and reading with the fifth grade; and the sixth grade had to take
him in for their class in history.

It was Peter Haskins who scratched his head with worri-
ment and asked, "How do they run schools in Ireland,
anyway?"

And Brian Boru had answered, "At the rate a lad can
learn and get on with his books."

By the end of the week the boys were teaching him to
play a game called basketball, with the promise of teaching him another game—a real yankee game called baseball
—as soon as school closed. The girls were beginning to

smile at him and to sit next to him in the school bus going home. Before the week was over, he was dropping his "lass" and "lad," and picking up American words fast, and the following week a wonderful thing happened—the school had a fine showing of pictures.

It was part of the history work, and all the grades came together and crowded into the rickety seats for almost an hour to watch and listen while one or other of the teachers read or told about the country they were seeing. A big screen was unrolled at the far end of the room. A machine that buzzed and showed the pictures was managed by the teacher, who did no talking; and all the windows were darkened so that the pictures would show sharp and clear. Already the school had had Holland and France, China and Denmark. To Brian Boru's great astonishment, the schoolmaster announced that the pictures for that day were to be about Ireland; and, with a boy newly come from that country, he thought it would be great fun to have Brian Boru Gallagher tell about it.

The whole school hurrahed. Never before had they had a boy or girl from anywhere but America come to school. It was both a proud day and a sorry one for the namesake of the great king. Peter Haskins let him read the printed descriptions that went along with each picture, and then add what he liked about them—if he knew more than the print told.

He did, for his granda had traveled the length and

breadth of Ireland and had told Brian Boru all he remembered. There were Killarney Castle and the lakes as blue as ragged sailors. There was the Blarney Stone on the castle in County Cork. There were the Giant's Causeway and the city of Dublin, with the fine statue of O'Connell, the Irish scholar and patriot. There were County Galway and the ragged cliffs along the sea; there were County Donegal, and the fort that had been lost by the O'Donnells, and the hills nearby—so he could almost point to Binn Ban and the boreen going up to where he lived. There were some fine pictures of the Cattle Fair in County Kerry—and, finest and best, there was a picture of Tara, and he could say with pride that the first Brian Boru had ruled there as High King over all of Ireland. This was the grand part of that day in school.

The sad part came when the pictures showed the small cabins, the rocky roads and pastures, the poor look of the people as they stood by their nets in the coves, or by their small potato patches, or with the one pig they could call their own. Volleys of questions were thrown at him, and, being an honest lad, he had to confess that great parts of Ireland were as poor as the pictures showed, that lads like himself lived in just that sort of cabin, with one room to it; that inside the cabins they cooked over turf on the hearth, and that they had no such finery as refrigerators!

It was Bill Bunker, the postmaster's son, who said, "Looks to me as if Ireland had nothing to boast of but a

bit of scenery. Don't tell us that America isn't ten times as big and rich a country."

"Boasting is bad manners," said Peter Haskins. And then he showed the last reel of pictures, and in that one was a Donegal schoolhouse. A great lump came into Brian Boru's throat. There it stood, white and pretty, with a fuchsia growing by the door, with primroses around the doorsill, and all of it as tidy and inviting as his very own schoolhouse on Binn Ban.

With the machine turned off and the windows un-
covered again, Brian Boru swallowed hard at the lump in
his throat and stretched his shoulders to make his skinny
body look almost as broad-beamed as the American lads'.
He spoke to the schoolmaster. "Mr. Haskins, sir, could I be
given a small turn at boasting and bad manners?"

"You certainly can."

" 'Tis well I'm knowing that Ireland is a poor country
besides America. But you'll find nowhere in the whole
world finer scholars, or people with more laughter to them,
more kindness. And even the poorest is a grand teller of
tales. A single man like my granda will know more than a
hundred tales of history and ancient kings, of adventures
and heroes—ay, and even of fairies. And the schoolhouse

you saw a while since could have been my very own. We keep them white and clean, and gay with flowers. Our schoolmaster, Tomas Teeney, is proud of it, as are all the la— the boys and girls who have gone there to get knowledge." His breath gave out suddenly, and he sat down.

A terrible silence filled the room. Full of fear lest he had lost all possible making of friends by his boasting, he looked around the crowded room at the faces turned toward him. He knew on the instant that every scholar there felt the same as he had on his first day about the ugly, dilapidated schoolhouse, the unkempt yard, the lack of anything pretty or gay. It made him ashamed of his boasting, and he made his apology as quickly as he could.

"You must know this as true, that in all of Donegal we

have no fine school bus to be fetching the scholars to school. We walk on our two bare feet. And never has Tomas Teeney had a machine for showing pictures."

The faces all around him that had looked so glum and solemn suddenly broke into smiles.

Peter Haskins patted him on the shoulder. "We're glad to hear we have something in Maine that we can be proud of. To tell you the honest truth, Brian, we're as ashamed of this schoolhouse as you are. For years we have been trying to persuade the township and our school board to build us a new one. But every year at town meeting the taxpayers vote against it. And we need new desks and new books— and more of them. We know what we need, don't we, boys and girls?"

A shout went up that filled the room. Brian Boru put a question. "Then why don't you have what you need?"

Again Bill Bunker took the floor. "Because a lot of old diehards get up every year at town meeting and say what was good enough for their fathers and grandfathers is good enough for us. That's why!"

Brian Boru spoke once more. " 'Tis a strange sort of poverty to be finding in a rich country."

And Katie Joy the schoolmistress said, "It looks as if it would take Aladdin and his wonderful lamp—or some sort of magic—to get us a new schoolhouse."

7. The Promise of Enchantment

THAT night after supper Brian Boru said to his Aunt Delia, "I have what they call 'homework' to be doing. With your leave I'll work in my own fancy room; and with your leave I'll take up a fistful of those fine cookies of yours and mug of milk—to be giving more power to my elbow."

But it was scant work he did. The fairyman came out of the top drawer in the chest where he had been making his bed, and sat down on the edge of the table. He knew the cookies and milk were for him, and before he asked any questions or started the usual night's blathering he munched and sipped, until his small wee stomach was full. At long last he asked, "What's put a stone on your tongue, laddy? And your face looks as sour as if you'd been eating green gooseberries."

" 'Tis thinking I am."

"Sour thinking never got lad or fairy anywhere. Don't be telling me ye are sorry ye came at all to this grand country. Think of all the lobsters there be's in it!"

"Ay and cookies, and all the milk we can drink. And a chicken for Sunday dinner, and fish and meat when we crave it. 'Tis a grand country; but it is ailing in school-houses, ailing badly." And Brian Boru went on to tell the fairyman about the one at Lobster Cove—along with the happenings of that day.

The fairyman swung one small leg over the other and pulled hard on his thinking lock. "I have an idea, laddy. It has just sprung at me."

Suddenly Brian Boru slapped the table with all the force he could put into one open hand. It raised the fairy-man a good five inches into the air, and he landed back on the table with a hard bump.

"I have an idea myself," said Brian Boru.

"You have my small wee bottom ruined entirely," said the fairyman. He rubbed it with great caution. Then he looked at the lad. "My idea is as plain as the nose on your

face. 'Tis the schoolhouse we will be laying an enchantment on."

"Ay, but could you make a fine new one by enchantment
in the place of the dirty one that is there, with its paint
peeling off and the doorsteps and underbeams looking
rotten?"

"I could not," said the fairyman. "I haven't so much
magic in me."

"Could you be after taking the boys and girls away by
enchantment—and maybe sailing the old schoolhouse off
somewhere?"

"I might; and then again I might not. It might be taking
help. But where I would get it, or how, I cannot be saying."

"You'd best listen to my idea. I got it from some poetry
the schoolmaster read to us a while since. It was a long bit
of poetry, and it was called 'The Pied Piper of Hamlin
Town.' It told a tale about a wandering piper who by his
piping rid a whole town of rats—big rats, small rats, large
rats, tall rats. He was to be given ten thousand guilders,
which is a lot of money. But with the rats gone, the townsfolk would not pay him. So he piped the children away. It
had a sad ending; but I'm of the notion we could make a
tale with a good ending."

Long they sat in silence, each thinking his own thoughts.
At long last the fairyman said, "I would have to be having
back my wee red cap."

"Are you an honest wee man, and would you promise to

do the enchantment first, before you wished yourself back in Donegal?"

"I would that. And to make it binding we could make the blood bond between us, same as in the days of old. Bare your arm, laddy, and I'll bare mine."

Brian Boru often had heard his granda tell of the blood bond made between kings and heroes. Likely King Brian Boru had made a blood bond, sworn his oath and kept it.

The fairyman rolled up the sleeve of his green coat; Brian Boru rolled up the sleeve of his wool shirt. The fairyman took the knife that belonged to the lad and that was always in his pocket. With help, he opened the smallest blade and, holding it like a cross-cut saw with his two hands, he made two slits in the lad's forearm.

"Take the knife and make the same in mine," he said. This the lad did. Then, by careful connivering, the wee man rubbed his bleeding arm against the lad's, saying, "Your blood and my blood, mixing as one blood, makes the bond between us. 'Twill never be broken; and all promises made must be kept—on your honor as an Irishman and mine as a fairyman." It was a solemn moment.

Brian Boru pulled up his wool shirt and unfastened the red cap that had remained pinned to him since May Eve in Donegal. He handed it solemnly to the fairyman. "The promise is kept by myself."

Solemn was the answer. "And the promise of enchantment made a while since will be kept by me."

Both had spoken in such loud voices that they brought the sound of feet coming up the stairs, and Aunt Delia's voice saying, "Whoever have you up there with you, Brian Boru, and you talking so excited?"

Never had the lad hidden anything so fast. He grabbed the fairyman and thrust him under the wool shirt. He pulled his sleeve down over the bleeding gash; and in an even louder voice than before he chanted, "Big rats, small rats, fat rats, tall rats. Black rats, brown rats—"

His Aunt Delia opened the door and looked about the room with very curious eyes. They searched every corner. They came to rest on the brown teapot which the lad kept on his chest of drawers. Aunt Delia picked it up, removed the lid, and looked into it, shaking it with care. Then her eyes met the lad's. "I hope you're a lad to be trusted."

"I am that, Aunt Delia. What you were hearing was myself, learning a poem. Every scholar has to recite something at the end of school."

His Aunt Delia sniffed. She was far from being satisfied. Her eyes left his and dropped to the bulge in his shirt. Should the fairyman wriggle or, worse still, should he feel himself suffocating and come up through Brian Boru's open collar for air—then the two of them and their fine plans would be lost entirely.

His Aunt Delia gave another, louder sniff. "I have a feeling you are hiding something from your Uncle Seumas and me. There's an odd feeling to this room since the first night you slept in it. Your uncle thinks you're up to some shenanigans, and I'm beginning to think the same."

No words found their way to Brian Boru's tongue. The best he could do was to open his eyes wide and look innocent of all shenanigans. His Aunt Delia gave a third sniff, went out the door, and closed it after her.

He waited a safe length of time, counting her steps down the stairs; then he pulled up his shirt and whispered, "Come up for air—if you're not choked entirely."

And with the fairyman sitting once again on the edge of the table, Brian Boru set his red cap firmly on the head that had been so long without its fairy covering and he said, "From this night you're as free as a bird. But I'm asking you not to leave me for too long at one time. I'm not used to a woman in the house—and my Aunt Delia has me twiggity."

The fairyman pulled himself up to his feet. "Open the window, laddy. I'm off to Donegal and my own fairy fort for the night. But I'll be back with you on the morrow."

Brian Boru flung the window wide. For an instant the fairyman stood, a grin covering his wee face entirely. Then he clapped his hands and shouted, "I'm for good old Ireland!" The next moment the table was empty—the fairyman was gone.

8. The Enchantment Begins

THERE was one week, and bit over, left of school, and much happened in that handful of days. Every night the fairyman was gone, but every morning when Brian Boru awakened he found the wee man fast asleep in the chest drawer, cuddled as snug as a kitten on top of his wool shirts.

For the most part the lad could get little out of the fairy-man as to how he was spending his nights—in Maine or in Ireland. That the wee man was up to mischief of some sort Brian Boru felt sure, for when he woke him to give him the food he had pilfered in the night from the refrigerator, the wee man opened his eyes with a wide grin and always said the same thing—"That piper in the tale you told a short while since—we have him beaten entirely. Keep your ears open and your mouth shut, no matter what happens."

And plenty did happen. Not a day passed that, once begun, a whispering did not start growing and spreading, until not a soul in all the cove was not leaning across the fence, or stopping a neighbor at the corner store, to tell of something amazing—wholly unbelievable, but nevertheless true, according to the words of this person or that.

First it was the Bunkers' cow. Bill's father kept two cows, and on Monday, when the boy had gone to feed them in their stalls, the brindle one had said as plain as if it had been his father speaking, "Bill, will you kindly give me more cow pellets?"

The next morning when the school bus arrived and the boys and girls were spilling out of it into the schoolyard, one of the Simpson's shoats, very pink and full of bounce, had come across the yard, singing, "For he's a jolly good fellow!" And he sang it straight at the schoolmaster.

It was that same day that Brian Boru's Uncle Seumas, and every other fisherman as well, came home with the

astounding tale that every lobster caught in their traps
was bright red—although they were all as lively as crickets.
Each man brought home that night two or more of the red
lively creatures so that their wives and neighbors would
not doubt them. To bewilder the townsfolk more, when
put in the pot to cook, every lobster turned a pale blue.
There were many people who would not eat them, but

those who did agreed they had never tasted anything with the flavor and tenderness of those red-blue lobsters.

Up in Brian Boru's fancy room he and the fairyman had a feast. " 'Tis a great pity," said the fairyman, "that I cannot be stopping longer in the Cove. We would be making it the most famous place for lobsters in all of America."

With several days of school still to go, strange things began to happen inside the schoolhouse. Up in the sixth-grade class, when Peter Haskins handed around the dirty, lop-eared books for reading, and told his students to turn to page 117, it was discovered that page 117 was blank—not a sign of printing on it but the number of the page. And when they all went skimming through the pages to find something that they could read, in the whisk of a small lamb's tail every page turned blank. It sent the boys and girls into delighted giggles.

The schoolmaster himself grinned. "It seems," said he,

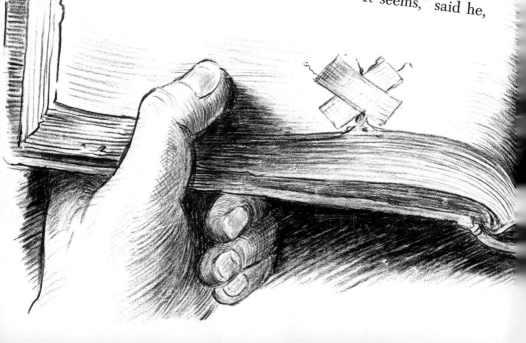

"that magic has come to Lobster Cove. It also seems that we can hold no class in reading today. Maybe Brian, from Donegal, Ireland, can fill in the time by telling us a tale."

"I can that. And I'll be making it one of my granda's best about the wee fairy people."

Not one tale did Brian Boru tell, but a bakers' dozen, with the next slipping onto his tongue as fast the one before slipped off of it. He told of the meal chests that had been filled in the famine years by fairy enchantment. He told of the music of enchantment that Conal the piper could play, and how he had played away and into the cabins of Binn Ban all the brogues the greedy cobbler of Donegal had made and was too tight-fisted to sell cheap to the neighbors, so each of them could have a pair to wear to his Great-aunt Brigit's wedding. He told of the enchantment put upon old John Hegarty's pipe, so that it never emptied as long as that fine old man had a breath left to draw with. And he told of the fairy cobbler—the leprechaun—the one fairyman in every fairy fort who knew where the fairy crock of gold was hid.

"My granda often told of how Danny McBride, who was storekeeper when my granda was a lad, once caught the leprechaun. 'Twas at the dark of the moon and he stumbled on him mending the fairy shoes, with his wee bench and all set up under a blackthorn, and a thousand fire bugs lighting him at his work. Danny caught him by the scruff of the neck, and keeping his two eyes fast on him, made him point to where the crock of gold was hid. 'Yonder,' said the wee man. 'Dig under yonder blackthorn and ye'll be finding the gold just under the crust of green earth.' Now Danny McBride was a knowledgeable man, and he said he would not let the cobbler go till he had taken his own green kerchief and tied it on a branch of the blackthorn the leprechaun had pointed out. Danny carried the cobbler over and held him aloft till he had the kerchief tied fast; then he let him go and went home to get a pick and shovel to dig with. A quarter-hour later, when he got back to the fairy fort, and had started across to where he was certain the blackthorn grew, he saw that every blackthorn bush for as far as he could see in the starlight had a wee green kerchief tied to it."

The boys and girls had sat spellbound while the tales were being told. Now Bill Bunker asked, "Did Danny never find the crock of gold?"

"Never. You can take it from me—the fairies can fool the humans every time, if they take the notion to."

Peter Haskins got up from his own desk and came over to where Brian Boru was sitting. "Tell me the truth, Brian, do they still have fairies in Ireland?"

"They do. But they've grown mortal scarce since the Yankee cornmeal has come over. They don't be liking it at all."

The schoolmaster put a firm hand on the Irish lad's shoulder. "Tell me the truth once more. Could it possibly happen that when an Irish boy came over to this country for the first time, he might bring with him an Irish fairy?"

Everyone listening could have heard a pin drop. Every pair of eyes was fastened on Brian Boru. He wriggled in his seat. He pulled hard on his thinking lock. He knew he had to tell the truth—but might he make the truth sound like half of a tale told?

" 'Tis this way, Mr. Haskins, sir. An Irish lad coming to this country might first have seen pictures of the grandness and magnificence of America, pictures of such things as tall buildings, parks, motorcars, and refrigerators. And it might happen that he cotched an Irish fairyman to fetch over with him so he could be showing that Ireland had something grand and magnificent like enchantment—something that America has never so much as dreamed of."

"I see." Peter Haskins said it very solemn. And at that moment—just to make certain that he did see—that very enchantment went to work. One rickety desk after another collapsed, sending the boys and girls sprawling on the floor. The only desk left standing was the one in which Brian Boru was sitting. Then, from high overhead, came the sound of invisible laughter, and with the laughter came good words in the north-of-Ireland brogue.

"There's a trick for ye. And there be's plenty more tricks to come after it." The laughter shot through the open window and faded out into the distance.

"School is dismissed," said Peter Haskins.

9. Hundreds and Hundreds of Wings

THE NEXT morning when the school bus drove into the yard the schoolmaster was there to meet it. He told the pupils that there would be no more school until the fall term opened. Vacation would begin a week ahead of the usual time. As the bus turned around to return the boys and girls to their homes, Brian Boru went up and down the aisle, whispering to each boy and girl, "Tonight meet me at the schoolhouse. Slip out quiet-like, so no one hears you. If you are after wanting a new schoolhouse, come every man's son and daughter."

Supper that night at his Uncle Seumas's was the only unpleasant meal he was to remember in America. There was still a feast of the blue lobsters, and as far as Brian Boru himself was concerned, they were more delicious than ever. He dipped each morsel into his cup of melted butter and savored it all the way down his gullet. But his uncle and aunt appeared to take small pleasure in the feast. Even his Aunt Delia's fine fresh biscuits went un-savored by them. Speech was wholly absent until the end of supper, when his Uncle Seumas seemed to take a sudden hold of his tongue.

He straightened in his chair and for the first time glowered at his nephew. " 'Twas luck at first I thought you fetched us. But a fine lot of luck it's turned out to be. You have the lobster business ruined entirely."

"Uncle Seumas, dear man that you are, how might I ever have done such a terrible thing?"

Before Seumas Gallagher could give him the answer, the two whole lobsters still left cooling on the platter suddenly laughed aloud, "Ha-ha-ha-he-he-heeeee!"

His Aunt Delia jumped from the table, turning over her chair. She clapped a hand over her mouth and went run-ning from the room as if a host of hobgoblins were after her. His Uncle Seumas got up with more dignity, but

Brian Boru could see that he was brimming with anger. "You see what you have done to your Aunt Delia. And if that were not enough, you have the whole town pointing a finger at us. The good name of Gallagher you have disgraced. Whatever you might have fetched over in the brown earthenware teapot I'll not be guessing; but this much I know—if your Aunt Delia and myself are ever to be looked on again as decent folk you'd best be leaving for Donegal the morrow. So pack your bag, my fine lad, and fetch the teapot back with you. 'Tis a sorry day your granda let you bring it over."

Never had the lad known anything but love and kindness from his uncle. He could feel a lump come up in his throat and tears welling into his eyes. Tears—for a lad his size! "Uncle Seumas, dear man that you are—"

"Don't you be saying 'dear man' to me!"

"But dear man—if you would but be holding your temper, and giving me a bit of your patience, and maybe leaving me stay a few more days and nights in the Cove, I could make you the promise that my Aunt Delia and yourself would never be sorry. I promise you the fancy shenanigans have almost finished themselves. Give me just a few more days, and you might not have to be paying my passage money back. Say it's a bargain, dear man!"

"Haven't I been long enough in America not to trust an Irishman with a bargain? He can wheedle the very heart out of you, and the last shilling out of your pocket."

"Your heart I have always had, Uncle dear. And I have small use of money—Irish or American, with all you give me. All I ask is a wee bit of time."

"Time you shall have. But I misjudge my own judgment." And Seumas Gallagher went out of the room, a down-daunted man.

That night the grownups of Lobster Cove must have been worn out by the happenings of the past few days to go to bed as early as they did. Long before half past nine the boys and girls were waiting for Brian Boru in the schoolyard. He came, hugging the brown teapot hard against his stomach; and in one hand he held the key to the door.

"How came you by that key?" asked Sammy French, the son of a lobsterman.

"It was easy to come by. Mr. Haskins, sir, keeps it over the door when he locks up. Now come inside. I have something to show the lot of you."

The boys and girls trooped inside after Brian Boru. To their wonder, all the desks and seats were back in their places. The pupils crowded into them, two to each seat, and Brian Boru, with the flashlight he had borrowed from his Uncle Seumas, stood at the head of the room and took off the lid of the teapot, holding the light steadily on it. A long, hushed breath was drawn in as more than fifty pairs of eyes beheld the small, wee figure of the fairyman come out, look about him a moment, and then sail over the heads

of those in the front rows and settle on the desk in front of Bill Bunker.

For a moment that boy's eyes popped with doubt at what he saw. Brian Boru reassured him. " 'Tis an Irish fairyman you're looking at. I fetched him over to put a bit of enchantment on America."

"He's been putting plenty on the Cove," said little Mary Crabtree.

The fairyman spoke now for himself. "It has all been just a bit of fun, a beginning, you might be saying, for the real business of enchantment."

"Meaning what?" asked Johnny Coombs.

"Meaning the schoolhouse," said Brian Boru. "You've all been setting your hearts on a new schoolhouse, and the fairyman and myself intend you shall have one."

"How?" a chorus of voices asked.

Again the fairyman spoke. "The how and the why of it can wait till tomorrow night. You'll all come again, the same as this very evening. Every lass and lad will fetch with him a goodish length of strong twine. Every lass and lad will fetch something in the way of eatables and drinkables—the lad here will tell you what. As for myself, I am off to Donegal to pick up a bit more enchantment—to do us till we have everything fine and fancy as a silver star."

He was there on the desk in front of Bill Bunker one moment; the next he was gone. Everyone sat spellbound while Brian Boru told them to be bringing cans of soup and cans of fruit and whatever milk anyone could fetch along, with what might be baked fresh and easy to eat from the pantry. "Fetch the full of your arms—for who knows how long we may be having to live on what you fetch."

The next night, again, the grownups must have bedded in and gone to sleep early, for the boys and girls were wait-ing at the schoolhouse with cans and pitchers, pails and dishes. Brian Boru came with a big pot, dozens of paper cups, and spoons for everyone. "We'll stack them, as Maine folk say, neatly on the teacher's desk. Did anyone think to fetch matches, for likely we'll need a fire." Five hands went up. "Now we will be waiting for himself, the fairy-man, to see what enchantment is brewing."

Every boy and girl had come barefoot, the better to slip out of the house without noise. Now under every seat toes wriggled ecstatically. Had they dared to turn on the lights it would have been seen that more than fifty pairs of eyes were sparkling with anticipated delight. Here they were, born and raised in Lobster Cove, State of Maine, U.S.A.— a place where minds could be as flat-footed and free of fancy as any to be found in the world. And yet, here they were, about to step into a living tale of fairies and enchant-ment—with even more to happen, for all they could guess.

Suddenly, for the second time in their lives, they heard the sound of high, shrill laughter above their heads. Then —as suddenly as before—there was the fairyman, in his green round-about and the red cap on his head, standing a man's-hand high on Brian Boru's shoulder. His face was wrinkled deep with that laughter. Fun sprouted out of his eyes and caught at his wee mouth, and he shouted in his loudest voice, "Are ye all set for the enchantment, lads and lasses?"

"We are—oh, we are!"

"Have ye fetched the twine?"

"We have!" And out of blue-jean and apron pockets came more than fifty neatly rolled balls of twine.

"The past days I've been spending with the sea birds along the water's edge and on the wee islands. I have been telling them of the hard times that have been overtaking the lads and lasses of the Cove, and of this poor, ugly, worn-out schoolhouse—not fit for a fine Maine lad to be learning his reading and writing in. And they have all agreed to help Brian Boru here to overcome this tremendous difficulty. Hark ye!"

Toes stopped their wriggling, ears were cocked.

"Open the windows and ye'll be hearing better," said the fairyman.

Every window was flung wide, and over the sill of every one crowded the children, until each window held four or five of them.

That was the moment that ears caught the rising sound of wings on the night air—hundreds and hundreds of wings, coming nearer. But the night being dark, and only the stars giving light, along with the few nearby street lights, the sound of wings was almost upon them before the watchers saw the birds. Gulls—seagulls, skimmers, black-back gulls, and herons, the great blue herons, their legs stretching half a yard back of them before they lighted on the ground under the windows. Last of all came four great bald eagles, their wings stretching seven feet across, and a great breeze from them striking the children as the birds swooped to the ground.

The fairyman took command. "The seven biggest, strongest lads, along with Brian Boru, will move desks to the two doors and brace them wide open. They must be made fast."

This was done, in the counting of a hundred.

"Now all the rest of you fill the windows. Throw out one end of your twine to the fine big birds waiting below. The other end make fast around your middles, and let every lass and lad see that the knots are square and strong."

This was done in the counting of another hundred.

"Now, ye eight big, brawny buchals, brace yourselves to the desks at the doors, throw out your twine, and fasten the other ends both about your middles and the legs of the desks." The fairyman made a hollow of his two hands and called, "Ye great, grand birds, ye American eagles that

do be marked on nearly every piece of silver money in the country—ye come and take the ends of the big lads' twine, two of ye to each end. For the rest—let as many gulls and herons as can take a firm hold do so!"

With wonder and growing excitement, the children gripped their lengths of twine, while the birds caught the other ends with their beaks. You could count as many as twenty birds to one end. At the front of the schoolhouse Brian Boru and the biggest boys watched the eagles take their twine. Not only with their great beaks did they take hold, but with their talons as well. A moment of hushed stillness covered the schoolhouse, as well as the whole night.

Then the fairyman soared as light as a small tern through the doorway and lighted on the back of one of the eagles. One hand caught fast to the neck feathers of the great bird; the other clamped the red cap firmly to his head while he shouted, "Clip clap, clip clap, I wish us all safely on Egg Rock."

It was like the rushing of great waters, that sound of the birds mounting into the air. Every child unconsciously braced himself against the tug of the twine. Slowly, with many creaks and splittings, the old schoolhouse broke loose from its rotten foundations. For a few breathless seconds it tipped back and forth, like a ship in a rough sea. But so absolute was the faith in the enchantment of all inside that not a sound passed any lips.

Up, up, up went the schoolhouse, floating after the birds. Another moment, and it had righted itself and was sailing through the air as evenly as ever it had stood upon the ground. Still not a word came from the children—only a long-drawn sigh of wonder.

10. The Wee Man Keeps His Promise

F OR ONLY the length of a long breath did the boys and
girls of Lobster Cove get a glimpse and a feeling of
the wonder of that flight. For an instant only, a half-grown
moon broke through the clouds and they could catch white
light on white wings and breasts, and the shadows of long
legs thrust out behind the herons. The schoolhouse moved
with the lightness and sureness of a bird in the air; then
the clouds had the moon again and the children could see
little. But they did feel a sudden, slow sinking, followed by
the grating sound of timber against rock.

The birds dropped their lengths of twine. Tidily the
children began to roll them up. The eagle who had carried
the fairyman sailed to an open window, alighted on the sill,
and stood huge and mighty as the wee man dropped off his
back. For a moment he stood on tiptoes, stroking the back
of the huge bird. Then with a sweep of his hand to all the

birds he shouted, "A thousand million thanks to ye. Off ye go—to your nests and your feedings!"

Every bird took the command; none of them but the eagles flew far. The children could hear the swish of wings for an instant; and then it seemed as if every bird had alighted close by.

This brought a laugh from the fairyman. "We have them filled with a great curiosity entirely. Having fetched the schoolhouse and the childher here, they want to see what next happens." He turned to Brian Boru. "Have I filled my end of the bargain, laddy? And if I have, can I be dandering off to Donegal?"

"You can not. You'll be staying, the same as myself, till we see how the enchantment works on the taxpayers and school board."

"And if I stay, might ye be coming back with me?"

"I might, and again I might not. Hold your questions till morning comes."

Brian Boru, with the boys and girls crowding the door-way behind him, stepped out into the night. As if the half-moon had joined the enchantment, she broke through the clouds again, so that everything about the schoolhouse was lighted brightly. All around were piled rocks, and below these ledges stretched out in every direction to the farther waters of the bay.

In chorus the children shouted, "We're on Egg Rock."

And Bill Bunker added, "Why, nobody ever comes here."

"That was my very idea, mine and the birds'."

"But however will our parents find us? We're lost, we're truly lost." Little Mary Crabtree began to cry.

The small ones began to snuffle ominously. Brian Boru knew that in a moment the whole promise of a fine new schoolhouse would be forgotten and he would have more than fifty heartbroken, keening children on his hands. He jerked the coat-tails of the fairyman beside him. "Speak up, wee man, and put sense and courage into the lot of them."

Again the fairyman took command, and with a brave shouting, "Harken ye! How many of ye have ever been on an adventure? And how many have dreamed of an adventure, and the bold, brave way ye acted when off ye went, like the King of Ireland's son, to seek it? Well, here ye are—all safe together, with the Irish laddy and myself to watch over ye—and likely the birds near enough to give a hand be they needed. 'Tis rarely the adventures that humans dream of ever come true. But here is yours. It makes the beginning of a fine tale ye'll have to tell your kinfolk while you're still young, and your childher when ye have grown old."

The snuffling stopped. Brian Boru took up the blathering. "Here and there you'll be finding some bits of grass and smooth places between the rocks. Each of you find yourself a soft place to sleep; and I'll lay a wager—the old schoolhouse against a fine new one—that come morning

we'll have all the boats in the Cove out here searching for you."

He could see that a few of the small ones were thrusting out quivering lower lips. But the older ones had caught on to their courage, and with hands over smaller shoulders they were leading the young children toward the dips in the rocks, whispering reassuring words. In no time at all they were snuggling down, an older with a younger, in some comfortable place.

The gulls and the herons, feeling that the children were still their charges, waddled and stalked up from the ledges. Some went hither and some yonder; but every child was visited. Every child heard soft, laughing sounds or gentle squawks said over him—for all the world like disturbed parents comforting them at bedtime. Altogether the sound was surprisingly hushing, and the smaller ones began a sleepy giggling, their spirits high again.

Having hushed the children off to sleep, the birds went on with their tending. They gathered up anything they could find for covering—dry grasses and seaweed—and heaped them over their charges. As luck would have it, the night was gentle, and the children slept the lee long night through.

They were awakened by a great shouting, a blowing of

foghorns, a ringing of ships' bells. The air was still warm, the sea was calm; and circling Egg Rock was a great gathering of boats: dories, dinghies, lobster boats, and fishing smacks. Each was crammed to its gunwales with fathers and mothers. Up from brush and rock crannies popped heads—fifty and more of them. Beyond the shoals that kept the boats at a distance came the shouting again. This time words could be heard. "Hi, there, Jimmy!" . . . "Sally, are you all right?" . . . "Johnny, wave to us!"

It seemed incredible to those parents, who had awakened at dawn to find their children gone, and had searched for them for hours by land and water, suddenly to find their lost ones full of laughter, and treating the whole terrible happening like a jolly adventure.

Seumas Gallagher, from his boat, hollowed his hands and shouted, "Brian Boru, stand up!"

Still heavy with sleep, head tousled, the lad from Ireland not only stood up, but nimbly as a goat leaped the rocks to the ledge that stretched farthest into the water. It brought him not fifty feet from his uncle's boat. "I am here, Uncle Seumas, dear man."

"Dare you not call me 'dear man,' you rascal. However you fetched the schoolhouse and all the childher out to Egg Rock, I'm not the man to ask you. But I do ask you, how will you fetch them back?"

"The schoolhouse—never! But this we promise—all the lads and lasses shall be fetched home again."

Bill Bunker's father, not only the postmaster, but a member of the school board, shouted, "We must have the schoolhouse back! Lobster Cove must have it!"

"It can build itself a new one. And you'd best put your heads together fast, for until the new schoolhouse starts building we stay here. If you want your sons and daughters home safe and sound, let us hear the sound of new ground broken, and the ring of hammers on timber. And pick a spot that is pretty to build the schoolhouse on, for the scholars and the teachers do be thinking there has been enough of ugliness."

The shouting used up all of Brian Boru's breath. Furthermore, he had said all that mattered. No schoolhouse, no children. It was like the Pied Piper with his ten thousand guilders.

The boats drew together, and Brian Boru could make out that there was a fashing and blathering among those in them. Let them blather. He called the boys and girls together and led them inside the old schoolhouse, where they set about making a fine breakfast.

The fairyman, who had slept through till dawn himself, now sent the birds to gathering driftwood; and soon a fine fire was going and the pot Brian Boru had brought from his uncle's house was slung over it between two poles stuck in the rocks. Into this they dumped all the canned soups: chicken-tomato-beef-celery-pea-mushroom. It sent forth a tasty smell as it hotted up. Everyone dipped into the pot with his own spoon; boxes of crackers were broken open. Not a word was spoken while soup and crackers went down more than fifty gullets. Everyone said it was the best soup mixture he had ever tasted. It put so much heart and spirit into the boys and girls that when their parents gave out a final shouting—"Are you certain sure you don't want to come home?"—the answer came in a gusty chorus, "No!"

After the soup, all the canned fruits were dumped into the pot; and again all voted it the best mixture ever. With this went cake: chocolate-layer, coconut-layer, lemon cream pie, and cookies. The fairyman was not forgotten. He began with soup poured into a paper cup nearly the size of himself. He ladled it out with a teaspoon, taking two hands to it, and all his muscle. Out of the fruit mixture he picked all the cherries and topped them off with a slab of chocolate cake so huge that Brian Boru begged him to leave half of it. But he finished it off, down to the last crumb, stroked his stomach benignly, and said, " 'Tis the tastiest, fanciest breakfast I ever put down me."

The children hardly noticed when the boats left. So full were they with contentment that Bill Bunker voiced for all of them what they were thinking: "I haven't a doubt but they'll be ready to start on the schoolhouse tomorrow. Once they quit their chawing, they'll get to work."

But the fairyman was of another opinion. "The older and more human folks grow, the more they blather. Blather,

blather, blather—then maybe they'll fetch pick and shovel and begin digging."

Even little Jerry French knew better than this. "They'll get the bulldozer over from the harbor."

"Whatever they start working 'tis myself better go and see they start. Likely I'll have to try my cap at more tricks." And with that he was gone, like a piece of thistle-down.

A wonderful performance happened toward sundown. The gulls gathered clams and dropped them down to the ledges fifteen to twenty feet below to crack them open. The boys and girls gathered them, washed them, and shucked them. Then they started another fire, and, having wiped out the big pot, in a manner of speaking, put the clams in with the last of the milk and made a fine stew. Even the big herons made their contribution. They waded out along the edge of the shoals and caught a lot of small pollock. These the boys with jackknives cleaned and scaled and, with the heads off, they were dumped into the pot to make a flavorsome mixture.

After that until dark they played a game, called, "Early Settlers," gleaned from old tales told by their grandparents. There were French, English, Indians, and a few who claimed to be the beginning of Americans. It was a bloody game, with lots of driftwood-tomahawking. In the end all were corpses but the beginning Americans who whooped their victory.

11. The Hero of Lobster Cove

AGAIN the night was gentle. Big and little together
snuggled down into the crevices or on the smallish
flat spots of sand and weeds. They waited with hushed
excitement to see would the birds come again. Come they
did, making the softest, most enchanting sounds, and carrying more bunches of dried grass, weeds, and seaweed. No
wonder the children dreamed of hosts of fairymen, of birds
that looked like their parents, some wearing blue jeans and
some sprigged aprons.

Meanwhile, throughout the late afternoon, things were
not exactly quiet at Lobster Cove. The fairyman, invisible,
listened to meetings held in the town hall by the taxpayers,
to meetings held in Peter Haskins' house by the school
board, and to meetings held by just parents in their own
kitchens. All he heard was words—words—words. Nothing
at all that sounded to him like plans for a new schoolhouse.

" 'Tis always money they are talking about. How much this will cost; how much that will cost." He mumbled it out of temper to himself. So then he set to work.

Cass Martin owned a small herd of goats. Suddenly they started bounding down the one main road of the Cove, each wearing a dunce-cap between its horns. And attached to the horns of the leading goat, and floating almost straight in the breeze, was a white banner with black words on it. The goats' frantic bleating brought all the people to the doorways and windows. Aloud they read the words: NO SCHOOLHOUSE, NO CHILDREN. Then the goats scattered as if hobgoblins were after them.

That started the dithers. Everyone went back to the meetings; but soon a loud caterwauling brought them again to the doors. This time, down the road scampered every cat in the Cove with her kittens. The caterwauling became plain words for everyone to hear: "We want a schoolhouse. We want a schoolhouse. We'll not catch a mouse till you build a new schoolhouse!"

This gave all the grownups further dithers. They tried to call meetings to order but the only sounds they could make were ridiculous: "Meou! Meou!"

All the hens out of the barnyards came next. They marched like soldiers, right-foot, left-foot, and they sang, "Cackle, cackle, cackle; that schoolhouse you'd best tackle. Not an egg will we lay if you don't build today."

But it was the cows' parade that really started Lobster

Cove going. They were all decked out in spring bonnets, with wreaths around their necks. One by one they came slowly, with great, solemn dignity. There was Jeb Tinker's Holstein, Bess; Postmaster Bunker's two Jerseys, Mill and Elsie; the Hazleton's Guernsey, Sal; and many more. Over the late afternoon breeze their voices sounded sad and urgent:

> "Moo, moo, a poor lot of humans, you!
> Not a quart of milk will we let down
> Till there's a new schoolhouse in this town.
> Moo, moo, moo!"

Everything was forgotten—meetings, money, lobster traps, meals—in a great longing for the children. Telephones were as busy as honeybees, buzzing. Two bulldozers were located and their owners agreed to begin work the next day. Lumber, tiles, roofing, kegs of nails, concrete by the ton, builders and masons and carpenters and handymen—all were arranged for. The whole of Lobster Cove tumbled into bed so worn out there was no more blather in them.

All the boys and girls on Egg Rock were still dreaming —that is all but Brian Boru. He twisted, he turned, the ground under him grew harder and harder. His mind whirled like a carousel, thinking. Nothing was left to eat but cake. Suppose the grown folks still could not make up their minds. Suppose the children, especially the smallest, got homesickness on empty stomachs. And—most upsetting of all—suppose the fairyman, this time, never came back. How would he ever get the children home?

He was saying over and over to himself, "There be's the blood bond between us. We both made the promise. He is a wee man of honor . . ." Suddenly he felt a twitching

of the lug of his top ear. The next moment he heard the well-beloved voice whisper, "Are you awake, laddy?"

Was he awake? Was he full of joy and cocksureness again? He sat up straight and saw by a moon more than half grown that the fairyman was grinning from ear to ear. "What luck, wee man?"

"My cap's full of luck. By sun-up tomorrow the whole of the Cove and the half of the county will be building the new schoolhouse."

"What do we do now?"

"I'm for getting back to Ireland before another night is clear gone."

"But first we must get the children back. We promised. How in the name of St. Patrick do we do it? Have you much enchantment left in the cap?"

"Not enough and to spare. I'd have to be going first to my fort in Donegal to fill it brimming."

"As bad as that?" Brian Boru sat back again, with a monstrous burden on his shoulders just as before the fairy-man had appeared.

"Not as bad as that at all—at all. Before I lighted the while beside your big lug I thought to be seeing yonder some buchaleen-bwee—same as what grows by the fort. We'll take a gander. If they be's enough stalks we'll give the childher a ride back on the fairy ponies."

Together they went; and how they blessed the moon! It was exactly as if she and the whole firmament shared the enchantment, for not a cloud darkened the sky. The fairy-man led the way, Brian Boru stumbling after him. They slid down an upper stretch of ledge to a wide stretch of growing things below. The fairyman set up a wee shout and the Irish lad set up a fine one. There was a whole forest of mullein stalks growing, enough to ride the boys and girls home.

Brian Boru had his jackknife out of his pocket in whisk of a lamb's tail. He cut close to the bottom, so each stalk could carry three or four along its length. It was stout mullein; and as he cut, the fairyman swung his leg over each, and there was as sleek and prancing a wee pony as heart could wish. Each he rode up to the crevices where the children slept. In each ear he whispered, "Hang fast to your dreaming. 'Tis of a fairy pony—who will ride you safe over sea and land till you be's snug in your bed." And with the loading of each pony he gave a gentle slap on its flank and shouted, "Each wee one to his own home!"

Before ever the moon set, the boys and girls were gone. Old, ugly, and deserted the schoolhouse stood in the last of the light. The fairyman and Brian Boru stood beside it. "The blood bond held," said the lad.

"The promise is kept," said the fairyman. He looked up at the lad beside him. "Might ye be staying—or might ye be leaving with me?"

"Would there be enchantment enough in the wee red cap to fetch the two of us to Donegal?"

The fairyman grinned again. "With ye in mind I did be saving one of the buchaleen-bwee. That, with the red cap, will fetch us as quick and easy as if we were riding one of the American rocking chairs your Uncle Seumas has in his house."

"What about the brown teapot?"

"We'll be after leaving that behind us as a remembrance —good or bad—the way they may be looking at it."

Brian Boru stood for a moment, pulling his thinking lock hard. He would never forget how kind had his uncle and his Aunt Delia been, nor ever forget the good things he had eaten—nor the wonder of a refrigerator. But he had missed his granda, Tomas Teeney, sir, and his schoolmates more than he had ever let himself believe. Oh, to see the

snug wee cabin again; and hear another fine tale by
candlelight; to be cutting down the boreen and across the
bog to school; and to hear his master call from the door,
"You're as welcome as the song of a throstle, Brian Boru.
Come in and learn to be a knowledgeable man!" Given a
few more years and it was not beyond his thinking that he
might become just such a fine Irish schoolmaster as Tomas
Teeney himself.

He let go his thinking lock with a jerk, as if it had suddenly held nettles. "I'm off with you, wee man!"

The next day Lobster Cove wakened to the sound of bulldozing, building, and blather. The plans for the new schoolhouse, drawn so long ago, were stretched on the ground with stones at the corners to keep them from blowing away. People forgot their usual chores, to stand around and talk of how much needed the new schoolhouse had been and of how fine it would be. In every home the boys and girls who belonged there wakened with a shout of surprise to find themselves in their own beds. Parents looked at them in grave puzzlement; but they never asked

how they had come home. There had been enough of
enchantment to last for generations.

Brian Boru was never seen in Lobster Cove again. But
he and the fairyman and the fairy ponies filled many a
dream, only to be forgotten entirely upon waking.

But a picture postcard came from Brian Boru at every
end of schooltime. The first one was a picture of the Giant's
Causeway. Carefully the lad wrote, "America is a fine country; but I'm still proud of Ireland and Donegal. I'm still
proud to be growing into an Irishman."

Among themselves the boys and girls of the Cove talked
often of the happening, and of Brian Boru; but never to
their elders. It was little Mary Crabtree who put into
words what all of them felt: "I think Brian Boru was a hero
—the same as that High King of Ireland he told about.
Likely he'll be the only real hero we will ever know."